A Rock
Against the Wind

A Rock Against the Wind

African-American Poems
and Letters
of Love and Passion

Edited by Lindsay Patterson

Foreword by Ruby Dee

A Perigee Book

Some of the material in this book previously appeared
in the original hardcover edition of *A Rock Against
the Wind,* published by Dodd, Mead & Company,
1973, copyright © 1973 by Lindsay Patterson.
See Acknowledgments, page 187, for further copyright information.

A Perigee Book
Published by The Berkley Publishing Group
200 Madison Avenue
New York, NY 10016

Copyright © 1996 by Lindsay Patterson
Book design by Irving Perkins Associates
Cover design and illustration by James R. Harris
Photograph of Lindsay Patterson on page 195 by Phyllis Cannon-Pitts

First edition: February 1996

Published simultaneously in Canada.

Library of Congress Cataloging-in-Publication Data
A rock against the wind : African-American poems and letters of love and
    passion / edited by Lindsay Patterson ; foreword by Ruby Dee.—Rev. ed.
        p.   cm.
    "A Perigee book."
    ISBN 0-399-51982-3
    1. American poetry—Afro-American authors.   2. Love poetry.
I. Patterson, Lindsay.
PS591.N4R63   1996
811.008'0354—dc20   95-30268
                                          CIP

Printed in the United States of America

10 9 8 7 6 5 4 3 2 1

With love to R. Rose, J.H. Clarke,
M. Angelou, E. Albee, O. Davis,
J.J. O'Connor and R. Dee,
who always came through
when I needed them

Contents

SECTION 4

Need/Want

Seduction

SECTION 6

Revelations

SECTION 7

Reflections on Lost Love

SECTION 8

Forever

SECTION 9

Letters of Love and Passion

Foreword

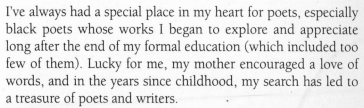

I've always had a special place in my heart for poets, especially black poets whose works I began to explore and appreciate long after the end of my formal education (which included too few of them). Lucky for me, my mother encouraged a love of words, and in the years since childhood, my search has led to a treasure of poets and writers.

Ossie and I were first introduced to *A Rock Against the Wind* more than twenty years ago when it became a delightful and invaluable reference and resource. We have quoted from it, been inspired and informed by it as we've traveled from campus to campus sharing "the word" with thousands of eager listeners. Now, with this second edition, Lindsay Patterson brings us yet another harvest of love poems from the best of our poetic voices. Some familiar: Angelou, Madhubuti, Rodgers, Cleage, Troupe, Giovanni, Walker, Randall—to name a few; others to be discovered and remembered through their fine contributions to this anthology.

I must warn you: this is not a book to be relegated to esoteric discussion, nor is it intended to sit, unattended or unread, on the coffee table or on that shelf we always mean to get to as soon as life and time allow. It is not meant to be skimmed or sampled, but rather to be savored, treasured, and most definitely shared. At midnight, in daylight, whispered, shouted. Taken as an antidote and a salve for wounded or broken hearts. A reflection in which you're sure to see your-self.

We need love poems now more than ever—when the metaphor of the rock against the wind has become more a boulder against a whirlwind of apathy and madness, of bitter-ness and rage that threaten to uproot and erase us. We need love poems *now*. In these rhythms and counter-rhythms we are beautiful; we are vulnerable; we are strong; we are possi-ble; we are gloriously (and shamefully) human. We need these bite-sized bits of love: new/old/true/low-down/forever/don't-love-you-no-more/woman/man love.

Here now, in ample supply, are our lyric griots, testifyin', sig-nifyin', pullin' coats—lifting the lamplight on love's horizon.

Ruby Dee
September 1994
New York

Introduction

Every Sunday afternoon in summer my family would attend three or four rural churches, and at each church my father would be called upon "to make a few remarks." At the end of his "remarks" he would often quote a poem that he had written. One of his favorites began: "Love and respect / Respect and love / That's what our hearts and minds / Should be fullest of."

My father was attempting to make the point that a people's survival depends upon truly liking and loving each other, for most of the worshipers in those rural Louisiana churches were sharecroppers who were facing an uncertain future because of farm mechanization. And it was love, more than anything else, that would sustain them, as it was love, more than anything else, that sustained our ancestors during antebellum time. Surely William and Ellen Craft would have agreed with this assessment, for in the decade before the Civil War, the couple fell deeply in love and with the permission of their owners (even though unions between slaves were not legal) married. They were, however, attached to different households in Macon, Georgia, and could only see each other when their masters consented. Both wanted desperately to live as a normal husband and wife and so they began to plot their escape from bondage.

Their plan was for Ellen (who had often been mistaken as a

member of her owner's family) to masquerade as the wealthy owner of a "great" plantation, while William would pretend to be her "faithful servant." Over several months, the couple purchased from different stores (so as not to arouse suspicion) the "proper" clothing of a prosperous plantation owner.

When the day of their planned escape arrived, William cut his wife's hair short, and she dressed in the garb they had furtively purchased. And since neither could read or write it was decided that Ellen would wear a poultice on her right hand and pretend that she was gravely ill with inflammatory rheumatism.

In Charleston, South Carolina, a steamship clerk insisted that Ellen sign her name, but she pointed to her poultice; and in Baltimore a railway ticket agent insisted that she present a certificate verifying that it was "permissible" for her servant to pass from the slave into the free states. Ellen, however, replied that she did not know such a certificate was needed, and indignantly added that she would not have been sold tickets to Philadelphia if there had been any "problem" about her servant.

But in Philadelphia the couple was advised that it would be safer for them in Boston and, for a time, life in Boston was almost idyllic. William found work as a cabinet-maker (his profession in slavery) and Ellen took in sewing, and both attended night classes to learn how to read and write. But in 1850 a more stringent Fugitive Slave Law was passed and the couple fled to England, where they were able to express their love for each other in safety and freedom.

Twenty years later William and Ellen returned to Georgia, where they purchased land and built a school and church. Their love for each other (and their people) had indeed sustained them, and blossomed, through the worst and best of times.

Southern plantation owners, however, often disseminated (for obvious reasons) falsehoods about the love, courtship, marriage and sexual practices of blacks. But promiscuity and adultery among slaves were severely frowned upon by slaves themselves. Courtships were often quite elaborate rituals, with "sweet-songs" being composed by suitors and love being celebrated in ingenious rhymes:

> Love is a funny thing
> Shaped like a lizard,
> Run down your heart strings
> And tickle your gizzard.
> You can fall from a mountain,
> You can fall from above,
> But the great fall is
> When you fall in love.

and . . .

> Hold my rooster, hold my hen,
> Pray don't touch my Grecian Bend.
> Hold my bonnet, hold my shawl,
> Pray don't touch my waterfall.
> Hold my hands by the finger tips,
> But pray don't touch my sweet little lips.

In formal poetry, George Moses Horton was the first African American to write extensively of love; and he did so hoping to raise enough money to purchase his freedom and emigrate to Liberia. Horton was a slave in Northampton County in North Carolina but was hired out as a janitor at the University of North Carolina in Chapel Hill, where students bought his poems for twenty-five to seventy-five cents to present to their loved ones. Yet, what was so truly remarkable is that Horton taught himself to read and, until he learned how to write, dictated his poems to university students, faculty members and others.

But unlike Frances E. W. Harper, the first African-American woman poet to write extensively of love, Horton was never popular with the free black public since his poetry tended to be esoteric and nonpolitical. Mrs. Harper was an abolitionist as well as an ardent supporter of women's rights, and many of her poems, like "A Double Standard" (published in 1895), reflected her feminist concerns:

> Crime has no sex and yet to-day
> I wear the brand of shame;
> Whilst he amid the gay and proud
> Still bears an honored name.

George Horton's primary concern was the purchasing of his freedom. Unfortunately, he did not gain it until Union troops swept through North Carolina near the end of the Civil War, and after his liberation Horton settled in Pennsylvania and wrote mainly religious stories for Sunday School publications.

Horton died in 1883, and ten years later a yet unbroken string of black lyric poets emerged, beginning with Paul Laurence Dunbar, and becoming firmly entrenched with James Weldon Johnson, William Stanley Braithwaite, Countee Cullen, Georgia Douglas Johnson, Angelina Weld Grimké, Helene Johnson and Langston Hughes. But it wasn't until after the turmoil of the nineteen sixties that black poets began to examine in specific and explicit detail the peculiar stresses and strains that had developed between black men and women from centuries of bondage and abuse.

And since the original edition of *A Rock Against the Wind* appeared in 1973, black love poetry has undergone yet another distinct change. In the original, many of the poems were concerned about the damage a hostile society had inflicted upon the emotional relationships between black men and women. But in this present edition most of the poems are far more personal, introspective and instructive about love. Even those poems which reflect on love lost supply advice about "getting on with your life," rather than becoming mired in tears, self-pity and defeat. And, as Ruby Dee indicates in her foreword, some of our finest poets are represented in this present edition; but also included (as in the original) are a substantial number of poets who are known only in poetic circles. The poems then were chosen for their content and wisdom, rather than the popularity or esteem of the poet.

While there has been a steady explosion in the writing of love poetry by African Americans, little attention has been paid to their love letters. Even though it was a criminal offense to teach slaves how to read and write, there were those who were taught surreptitiously by whites, and many more (like George Moses Horton) who taught themselves. Literate or not, a slave still had little control over his love life, as is apparent in this heartbreaking letter by Milo Thompson to his fiancée:

Miss Louisa Bethley:

I have got greatly disappointed in my expectations on next Saturday. I will be compelled to disappoint you at that time but I regret it very much. Master says I must put it off a little longer, until he can see farther into the matter. He says probably Mr. Birney may break up house keeping or something of the kind and he don't know what may become of you, for that reason we must defer it a little longer. I will come up and see you shortly and then we will make some arrangements about it. It is with great reluctance that I put it off any longer, but I am compelled to do it owing to the circumstances I have related. I shall remain your affectionate lover until death.

Milo Thompson

In *A Rock Against the Wind* there are contemporary letters (and poems) that celebrate love between men and women and explore the love between parent and child. Of course the reason African Americans will continue to celebrate and explore love in prose and poetry is most aptly expressed by poet Saundra Sharp when she declares,

We still write love poems
because in the deepest
most resonant part
of our collective spirit
We won't let love
be taken away from us.

and

because it keeps hate
from getting out of hand

*and most
important of all*

because it [love] heals us. . . .

A Love Poem

I do not expect the spirit of Penelope
To enter your breast, for I am not mighty
Or fearless. (Only our love is brave,
A rock against the wind.) I cry and cringe
When the cyclops peers into my cave.

I do not expect your letters to be lengthy
And of love, flowery and philosophic, for
Words are not our bond.
I need only the hard fact
Of your existence for my subsistence.
Our love is a rock against the wind,
Not soft like silk and lace.

ETHERIDGE KNIGHT

A Rock
Against the Wind

To Be in Love

A Small Contradiction

It is politically incorrect
    to demand monogamous
        relationships—

It's emotionally insecure
    to seek
        ownership of
        another's soul—
            or body   &
damaging to one's psyche
to restrict the giving and
    taking of love.

    Me, i am
totally opposed to
monogamous relationships
        unless
            i'm
            in love.

        PAT PARKER

Haiku

when i felt your warm
touch, i swelled up until the
streets were filled with you.

SONIA SANCHEZ

To Mareta

I miss you now
as always
and as always
I know
that the time
spent with you
is not time enough
and that
there can
never be TIME/enough

remembrances of early mornings
of waking still hugged from the night before
and you are asleep
and I am lonely.

that is perhaps selfish.

I know.
but I want every moment to be our moment
every dream our dream
every breath our life
every touch without separation.

for love
you are just that

and it is you
that completes me

> I think of afternoons
> and it is autumn
>> or perhaps spring
> and even if it is winter
>> it is yet summer
> because all thoughts
>> of afternoons
>>> are thoughts of you
> and all thoughts of you

are warm thoughts
> yes love
they are
> warm thoughts

it is nightfall
> and the stars have yet to make their appearance

but the moon is out/ALREADY
yes love

> the darkness is you just as the light is
> just as summer winter fall spring all are

you

> and I think
> and you are
> and I dream
> and it is your fantasy

MARETA

your name
a fantasy as real as touch
as true as I love you
mareta/FOR
you are my life
as the sun's glow
is the tree's green

as you/me/I/you/we are US
experiencing the experience
of being
of knowing the importance/TO BE
TOGETHER

HERSCHEL LEE JOHNSON

Reply

I cannot swear with any certainty
That I will always feel as I do now,
Loving you with the same fierce ecstasy,
Needing the same your lips upon my brow.
Nor can I promise stars forever bright,
Or vow green leaves will never turn to gold.
I cannot see beyond this present night
To say what promises the dawn may hold.
And yet, I know my heart must follow you
High up to hilltops, low through vales of tears,
Through golden days and days of sombre hue.
And love will only deepen with the years,
Becoming sun and shadow, wind and rain,
Wine that grows mellow, bread that will sustain.

NAOMI LONG MADGETT

My House

i only want to
be there to kiss you
as you want to be kissed
when you need to be kissed
where i want to kiss you
cause it's my house
and i plan to live in it

i really need to hug you
when i want to hug you
as you like to hug me
does this sound like a silly poem

i mean it's my house
and i want to fry pork chops
and bake sweet potatoes
and call them yams
cause i run the kitchen
and i can stand the heat

i spent all winter in
carpet stores gathering
patches so i could make
a quilt
does this really sound
like a silly poem

i mean i want to keep you
warm

and my windows might be dirty
but it's my house
and if i can't see out sometimes
they can't see in   either

english isn't a good language
to express emotion through
mostly i imagine because people
try to speak english instead
of trying to speak through it
i don't know maybe it is
a silly poem

i'm saying it's my house
and i'll make fudge and call
it love and touch my lips
to the chocolate warmth
and smile at old men and call
it revolution cause what's real
is really real
and i still like men in tight
pants cause everybody has some

thing to give and more
important need something to take

and this is my house and you make me
happy
so this is your poem

NIKKI GIOVANNI

For a New Love

Love has come
Unexpectedly
And truth filled:

It has torn open
Closed places
That no longer
Need hiding spaces
Now that love has come
Unrushed
Building gentle joy
Wisps in new places,
And in new spaces
It was worth
Waking for.

CICELY RODWAY

Poem No. 11

yo/smile
green as an African morning
makes me turn
into a nite song
                    singen soft rhythms.
yo/smile
green as the laughter
i bring you
            rekindles me
and i burn
        as i trail black fire behind me.

SONIA SANCHEZ

Untitled

He
came
quietly
    like a soft breeze
    like a warm whisper.
He
slipped
inside
    my head
and
    began
    to turn
    the pages.
He
pressed
    his heart
against
    my heart
    his smile
against
    my smile.
He
sat
down
in the
    middle

of my
      soul
And
Christmas
came
early.

      C. TILLERY BANKS

When I'm Close to Carol, I Gotta Move...

My
Heart
becomes
an
African
drum
Sending
Snap
to my
fingers,
and
Boogie
to
my
feet . . .

RICHARD D. GORDON

Song in the Night

When the light has gone
and the trees have opened their arms
to the stars,
when the birds have packed
their songs away,
the music you hear
will be me
singing to you
in the night.

IRMA McCLAURIN

A Hymn to Black Men and Women

Love Song

Beloved,
I have to adore the earth:

The wind must have heard
your voice once.
It echoes and sings like you.

The soil must have tasted
you once.
It is laden with your scent.

The trees honor you
in gold
and blush when you pass.

I know why the north country
is frozen.
It has been trying to preserve
your memory.

I know why the desert
burns with fever.
It has wept too long without you.

On hands and knees,
the ocean begs up the beach,
and falls at your feet.

I have to adore
the mirror of the earth.
You have taught her well
how to be beautiful.

HENRY DUMAS

Plagiarism for a Trite Love Poem

you talked of the sun and moon
while i sat,
supportin my chin with my thumbs
and i thought of two stars, your eyes.
you expounded and pounded,
paced and raved
about fire and ice and the world's certain doom
and i was sure you were warmth,
you spelled out what was wrong with the brothas and
i pretended i understood
      (that's when i noticed your lips)
you explained "the wite boy" your hands shavin the
air as though in uh fight or some crucial hurry
and i silently agreed
then you spoke of the need for Black Unity and
i said yes.
      (and you kept on talkin) and
i said yes.
      (and you paused and listened) and

i
said
yes . . .

    CAROLYN M. RODGERS

Black Woman, You

You move as if there were always
music playing/somewhere, touching
your inner most ear like a feather,
with you in perpetual dance,
and I love it.

You speak as though every phrase were
from a love song, and every word were
a drop of dew on a morning sunlit field,
and I go crazy over it.

You make love as though it was
an art form created in your dream
one lovely spring evening, while
the world wasn't around,
and I praise you for it.

Black woman, my beautiful angel being
from heaven's hideaway place,
I love you for all that you are,
and I love you for simply being you.

CLAY A. FIELDING

Soul Sister

(for Marie Kelly)

I'm sure
we were friends
before we met,
and that
some measure
of what I am,
comes from you.

On a distant star,
our souls,
each with a single
virtue, must've
touched and drew,
one from the other,
a quality not common
before.

Your gift
mingled with
the essence of me
and created
a new sensation
to share.

I gave you tears,
you gave me laughter.
I gave you peace,
you gave me honesty.
I gave you courage,
you gave me humility.

We touched, and
like electricity
giving up sparks,
we grew in character
until we approached
being born.

We hitched a ride home
on the same comet, but
touched earth at separate
times.

We knew nothing
of our times before,
until our paths crossed
and our eyes met.
I Knew
I was your Brother.
In the instant
our eyes touched,
our hearts exchanged
another gift.

≫ RICHARD D. GORDON ≪

I Love You

I love you for the way in which your
    softness reaches into my most
    secret chambers not disturbing
    the sleeping blackness.

I love you for the way our dreams mix
    with artistic arrangement, glowing
    with a soft, textured light not
    comprehended by rational thought.

I love you for the times when we are not
    doing anything but just listening
    to our silence speaking of poignant
    moments.

I love you for what we are to each other
    now, not in some distant time spectrum,
    and if our love can swim upstream
    against the current odds, so be it.
    If not, we will continue to journey
    inwardly.

I love you when our whispers are resonant
    with beautiful music yet unwritten.
    But most of all, I love you because
    we share the impossible and you call
    me friend!

BERNARD V. FINNEY, JR.

Infinity

What I really want to express is emotion.
What I'm feeling so full of is love.

How do I let you know my love?
I can tell you simply that I love you in infinite ways:
I love your constant communication with me.
I love your patience and understanding.
I love your energy and your eagerness as you enter each day.
I love the goodness in your heart that touches so many people.
I love the sincerity in your commitment to your work.
I love your concern for freedom.
I love your creative genius.
I love your faithful friendship.
I love your beautiful eyes, your expressive hands,
    your warm smile, your strong arms that caress me gently.
I love . . . I love . . . I love . . .
This is love in infinite ways, so there is no need
    to try to finish that which has no ending.

PHYLLIS M. BYNUM

Poem No. 21

if 'Trane had only seen
her body
and the way it smoothed
the brown light and
sent color to
the edge of darkness
as if it were the perfect
hands of some painter
he would have named it
with his horn
something vibrant and
unexplored, something loud
and still as someone
first touching their blackness.

DOUGHTRY LONG

Man Thinking About Woman

some thing is lost in me,
like
the way you lose old thoughts   that
somehow seemed unlost at the right time.

i've not known it or you many days;
we met as friends with an absence of strangeness.
it was the month
that my lines got longer & my metaphors softer.

it was the week   after
i felt the city's narrow breezes rush about
me
looking for a place to disappear
as   i walked the clearway,
sure footed in used sandals screaming to be replaced

your empty shoes (except for used stockings)
partially hidden beneath the dresser
looked at me,
as i sat thoughtlessly   waiting
for your touch.

that day,
as your body rested upon my chest
i saw the shadow of the

window blinds   beam
across the unpainted ceiling
going somewhere
like the somewhere i was going
when
the clearness of yr/teeth,
& the scars on yr/legs stopped me.

your beauty: un-noticed by regular eyes   is
like   a blackbird resting
on a telephone wire   that moves
quietly with the wind.

a southwind.

⋙ HAKI MADHUBUTI/DON L. LEE ⋘

When Sue Wears Red

When Susanna Jones wears red
Her face is like an ancient cameo
Turned brown by the ages.

Come with a blast of trumpets,
    Jesus!

When Susanna Jones wears red
A queen from some time-dead Egyptian night
Walks once again.

Blow trumpets, Jesus!

And the beauty of Susanna Jones in red
Burns in my heart a love-fire like pain.

Sweet silver trumpets,
    Jesus!

LANGSTON HUGHES

Nobody Says Baby

(for Robert G. Wells, 1942–1981)

it squirts from the coupling of colourful lips
like a seam in a pipe that suddenly rips

it slides from their lips in a sexy way
like unchecked passion in the middle of day

it shoots from their throats like a fired missile
pleasing the ear with a deep soulful sizzle

it steams from their sweet mouths as liquid love
sensuous, honeyed, like manna from above

its pure cadence makes me a womanly melt
too eager for loving so wantonly felt

nobody says it quite like them
nobody says "baby" like black men.

BEVERLEY WIGGINS WELLS

Poem

you said.
don't write me
a love poem,
but i would like to
creep across
yr shoulder and
whisper poems into
yr ear.
soft and black
moist and black
beautiful and black—
Strong.
rubbing my body
against yr chest.
Black.
and when you
ask me
why
i am so quiet.
it is only because
the poem sits
smiling
just
behind my lips.

PEARL CLEAGE

Poem for Joyce

my words are sad notes best tossed aside
    against the day when the Trashman comes to pick up
        trash.
remember me for my words for they are all I have
    in this world of ours, this land of plenty where the
government can dump millions of dollars of wheat
    into the sea.

remember me for my words, Joyce,
    for they are all that I can give you.
I don't have to tell you that I'm poor.
    we both know that, and more, as quiet as it's kept.

I'm poor, yes, and I'm black, yes, and I live in the ghetto
    yes, but that don't, no, it don't give me no complex
you see, Joyce,
    if I wanted to, I could be pretty and fancy and all that.
I could sit back in a chair for hours
    and talk to you, if nothing else, then just about
what it really means to have someone like you
    sticking here in my corner knowing that I'm down and
        out.

don't really care to cop a poor mouth,
    cause that really ain't where I'm coming from.
don't care actually to keep fronting
    like I got something and I ain't got shit worth counting.

Joyce, I ain't got nothing, Baby,
    I ain't got nothing to offer you but me.
I love you, Joyce,
    I love you so much until sometimes it scares me.

I sit and I think and I stare at you
    and when I think that you might be staring at me
why, I get shamed and start blushing and going through
        changes
        no other girl under the sun done ever put me thru.

I mean,
    like I don't go out of my way looking for trips to go on.
cause the world has got enough of those to go around.

you know what?
    it comes to this:
me, by myself now,
    and it ain't nobody looking over my shoulder making me
        write this poem to you.
    it ain't nobody that done asked me if I ever wrote any
        love poems.no.it ain't none of that kinda funny-style
        shit.
this is me.
    nothing, if you want to see me that way.
but this is me.
    and I see now that I'll never love another.

let me be sweet to you.
    let me be good to you.
let me hold you, yes!
    let me hold you and squeeze you,
or maybe even just touch you,
    but just let me do that
and I'll be just fine.

know what, Joyce?
    know what I saw yesterday
while I was out in those streets
    begging pennies from lint-lined pockets
playing the role of the puppet-sized gourmet
    at a wine-stained oaken table and generally
just tripping out very heavy
                        had you on my mind alla da time.
                        thinking bout you, bout how nice
                        it would be to come home to you,
                        to come to your loving arms and
                        go to sleep happy cause if I ain't
                        got nothing else at least I got
                        my woman.
thass why I'm writing you this poem, Joyce.
    because there's a lotta times when I get hung-up,
yes, get hung-up in a whole lotta bullshit
    that don't no kinda way make no sense and you and I
        both
know it,
            (but you let me slide,
            let me ease on off for the next day)
listening to my footsteps hollowly echoing
    dark the alleyway down the alleyway there I go
not quite being able to see what's right in front of me
    but moving on ahead anyway cause thass the bizness
a man's gotta involve hisself inta nowadays otherways,
                                        Missy,
it ain't too much that really means anything.

not people.
not money.
not fine homes or long cars or who got the most bombs.
not none of that shit.
not you.

not me.
not nothing, Baby, but what we got going for ourselves.

I want more than just the Blues, Joyce.
I want my Baby. I want Her Love, Her Tears, Her Happiness.
I want to make my Baby happy. I want to make you
     happy.
Will you make me Happy, too?

✂ JOHNIE SCOTT ✂

You Come to Me

you come to me
during the cool hours
of the day bringing
the sun; if you come
at midnight, or at two
in the morning, you come
always bringing the sun;
the taste of your sweetness
permeates my lips and my hair
with the lingering sweetness of Harlem
with the lingering sweetness of Africa
with the lingering sweetness of freedom;
woman, eye want to see
your breast brown and bared,
your nippled eyes staring,
aroused-hard and lovely;
woman, eye want to see
the windows of your suffering
washed clean of this terrible pain
we endure together;
woman, eye want to see
your song filled with joy,
feel the beauty of your laughter;
woman, black beautiful woman,
eye want to see
your black graceful body

covered with the sweat of our love
with your dancer's steps to music
moving rhythmically, pantherlike
across the african veldt;
woman, eye want to see you
naked, always in your natural beauty;
woman, eye want to see you
proud; in your native land

⌦   QUINCY TROUPE   ⌦

Chocolate Man

Loving chocolate fingers caressing my face
Strong chocolate arms circle in an embrace.

Honey, sugar, baby so fine and brown
You should have a kingdom and a crown.

You symbolize the best in men
Those of today and way back then.

When you look at me with those deep dark eyes
You make me want to bake you cookies and pies.

You make me want to sing and even shout
You make me want to see what life's all about.

I'm proud of the way you respect yourself
And never try to put me back on a shelf.

You are not afraid to do what must be done
Yet, you have a sense of humor
And you're lots of fun.

You are plainly so terrific in whatever you do
That is why my chocolate man
I'm so in love with you!

PHYLLIS M. BYNUM

It's a Boy!

Come, darling,
See what our love made,
The soft, black curls,
The wide, brown eyes
so like yours.
How they shine!
That speck of a nose
that will be pug like mine.

Look, darling,
See what our love did?
The plump, brown fingers
That grip your thumb
with such strength,
yet so gently,
Like your hands
When they caress me.

Come, da da,
Tickle his tummy,
And watch the gummy
grin that follows,
The toes that wriggle, then repose.
A genius! Should we
dare suppose?

Come, darling,
and see ourselves reprised
in a love
fully realized.

MICKI GRANT

Advice/Wisdom

New Blues from a Brown Baby

Some of my loneliest hours have been with you.
But now I know what I have to do.
Got to stop being your mother,
Stop looking down at you.
Got to stop being your teacher,
You'll learn for yourself what is true.

Some of my bitterest tears were because of you
But now I'm laying down a new set of rules.
Gonna stop being your sister,
'Cause you treat me like a second hand toy.
Gonna stop being both Miss and Mister
'Cause that kind of woman knows no joy.

I'm gonna take those lonely hours,
Push 'em way in the back of my mind.
I'm gonna take those bitter tears,
Turn 'em into smiles as sweet as wine.

And when you come home at night,
Ain't gonna find no mother or sister there—
You gonna find some hot! yet gentle loving
Like the answer to a special prayer.

And when something's troublin' your mind
You'll want to come and tell it to me.

Then we're gonna sit down and talk
Until I really get to know you, and you know me.

You're gonna have a new brown baby,
Gonna be all the woman I can be,
'Cause it's time,
'Cause it's just about time . . .

This is the last blues, daddy,
That you'll ever hear from me,
'Cause it's time,
'Cause it's way past time . . .

Won't be nothin' but sweet brown sugar
Melting all over you,
'Cause it's time for a new me,
'Cause it's time for a new we,
'Cause it's time . . . . . .

SAUNDRA SHARP

Nesting

Make a nest
a love nest

feather it
feather it with patience
    learn to wait
    avoid feeling the small hurts
   feather it with gifts of love
but do not overgive

feather it with softness
    soft evenings
    soft poems
    soft you
    be the ultimate diversion
            (from TV)

feather it with laughter
    your smile so shines
    that its absence is regretted

feather it with vibes
    of love
    of getting there
    of knowing/
            learning

          good cookin' vibes
        flyin' high with
      sweet wine & love time vibes

Make a nest
a love nest

    then wait,

for the sweet wild one
to find his way home.

         SAUNDRA SHARP

Love – The Beginning and The End

(intra means within)

the first aspect is love
is the Black Man and Black Woman
intragether.

        We have not yet learned to
hear, each other's inner voices, nor
move, within the rhythm of each other's pulses
     had not yet
cared to understand the gropings of
   one to the other. . . .

Black Man
        move into a Woman
        rush into her
scatter your seeds, plant your dreams
in her
     and you
        Black Woman
               open open
your self, open & bare your
softest fear, your nakedest secret
     open open to flow
intras-two into ones to hundreds to thousands

open Black Woman, open Black Man
W
O
M A N
A
N

the last aspect is Love.

CAROLYN M. RODGERS

Never Offer Your Heart to Someone Who Eats Hearts

Never offer your heart
to someone who eats hearts
who finds heartmeat
delicious
but not rare
who sucks the juices
drop by drop
and bloody-chinned
grins
like a God.

Never offer your heart
to a heart gravy lover.
Your stewed, overseasoned
heart consumed
he will sop up your grief
with bread
and send it shuttling
from side to side
in his mouth
like bubblegum.

If you find yourself
in love
with a person
who eats hearts
these things
you must do:

Freeze your heart
immediately.
Let him—next time
he examines your chest—
find your heart cold
flinty and unappetizing.

Refrain from kissing
lest he in revenge
dampen the spark
in your soul.

Now,
sail away to Africa
where holy women
await you
on the shore—
long having practiced the art
of replacing hearts
with God
and Song.

ALICE WALKER

Ballad

(after the spanish)

forgive me if i laugh
you are so sure of love
you are so young
and i too old to learn of love.

the rain exploding
in the air is love
the grass excreting her
green wax is love
and stones remembering
past steps is love,
but you. You are too young
for love
and i too old.

Once. What does it matter
When or who, i knew
of love.
i fixed my body
under his and went
to sleep in love
all trace of me
was wiped away

forgive me if i smile
Young heiress of a naked dream
You are so young
and i too old to learn of love.

⊲⊲ SONIA SANCHEZ ⊳⊳

Love after Love

The time will come
when, with elation,
you will greet yourself arriving
at your own door, in your own mirror,
and each will smile at the other's welcome,

and say, sit here. Eat.
You will love again the stranger who was your self.
Give wine. Give bread. Give back your heart
to itself, to the stranger who has loved you

all your life, whom you ignored
for another, who knows you by heart.
Take down the love letters from the bookshelf,

the photographs, the desperate notes,
peel your own image from the mirror.
Sit. Feast on your life.

DEREK WALCOTT

Moat

*(For Sallye & Robert . . .
on their wedding day, January 1, 1994)*

Stack
all your demons
on your outside porch
where torrents of
new and windy love can
drive them out of reach . . .
Then mold your Joy
into a river
that only Love
can cross . . .

RICHARD D. GORDON

On Learning

You have taught me how to dress without
awakening the whole world
I
have
learned to tip-toe quietly
out
of
love-filled nights
into
tomorrow's daily routine
and,
you have taught me to smile
half days
because
whole days are not up for grabs
and
I
want
to
Thank you, baby,
for teaching me how to leave gracefully,
without stirring the neighbors
or kicking your cat

MAE JACKSON

Free Yourself

Let go
of the old hurts
that keep you pinned down
closed in.

Release
the vengeance
that makes you
the victim.

Live
Breathe
New Life
New Hope
New Joys.

Yesterday's sorrows can only make you weak.
Nourish yourself instead
with love and forgiveness—
beginning with yourself.

Let go
and Free Yourself

Fly above it all
And soar in the peacefulness

Of a new found inner space—
That is controlled
By You.
For You.

Free Yourself
and Be Happy.

C. TILLERY BANKS

Let Go and Love

let go
and love.
extend yourself
beyond the boundaries
of your fears
        and touch
        and be touched.
no, life carries no guarantees,
—no 60-day warranties/
and yes, you may have been hurt
and you may be hurt again;
but in pain is progress
lessons learned,
gold stars earned
and joy, my love,
is but the prerequisite
of a soul-cleansing sorrow/
and sorrow but the prerequisite
of a soul-renewing joy.

let go and love.
reach out beyond
the limits
of the lower extremities
of your human being-ness.
  merge with/ touch

the invisible.
experience a spiritual orgasm
that lasts for
eternities.
                    reach me.
i am searching
for the infinity
of you.
            jammed into dark
            inner recesses
pondering future fears
past tears.
you elude me, baby.
please let go
and love.

i promise
i will be
gentle
with your
            soul.

⋈   LINDA COUSINS   ⋈

Drinking Beer

sometimes i watch
my new lover
drinking beer
on the side porch
with my old lover.
i listen to them laughing
and am amazed
at what the truth can do.

this is the payoff
for all those months
of struggling not to lie
even when i had no words
for what i felt
or thought or did
or needed to feel
or think or do.

all those months
of bravely stated theories
about monogamy being
the death of love
and the necessity of freedom.
all that shuttling between them,
full of guilt and tears
while they crossed their fingers

and waited for me to choose,
to send one packing
and take the other
home to momma,
but that's never been my style.

i'd rather let the moon decide.
i'd rather watch them laughing,
standing on the side porch,

drinking beer.

      PEARL CLEAGE

For a Black Lover

no, lover
holding is not enough
but touching is
touching eyes
touching lips
touching thighs
          which
if the stars
are right
& the moon's groovy
should lead
to the most important
connections
of all
          touching
hearts & minds
no, lover
holding
just ain't it
but touching is.

LINDSAY PATTERSON

SECTION 4

Need/Want

Relationship

I need to be with me now
I need to let myself love me deeply
Care for me tenderly
Help me carefully
I need to take me in my arms
Rock myself into a deep sleep
And rest until my spirit rises
Renewed and willed for a work
Long overdue

SANDRA SAN-VIKI CHAPMAN

I Am Somebody

I. I. I say I am. I say I am somebody.
Somebody because—because you—you make me—Somebody,
Because—because you are part of
Because you—you share the—the Somebodiness of me.

When you laugh, you make my lips a part of laughter.
When you cry, tension pulls me from inside.
When you are hungry, my food turns to poison makes me burst
Bony fingers clutch my tongue when I—when I know your thirst
Because you are part of—because you—you share the
The Somebodiness of me.

When I see your precious blood out of place, your bones exposed
    in death—
My blood chills and stops as I try to—try to—give you
    breath.
I must keep you from all fear and danger—
I must woo your peace of mind—
Help you—help you find joy—
Help you—help you find release
Because you are part of—because you—you share the
    the Somebodiness of me.
I cannot own that which you cannot also possess.
Your crime is mine, and from now on I'll confess
Because you are part of—because you share the Somebodiness
    of me.

You are at the other end of the steel spring of hate,
So I cannot hate.
When you know my love—my love will warm you—cleansing
    deep
So, let me—let me take your hand. Let me touch your fingers,
Feel your face. Know your heartbeat and all—all your
    doubts erase
Because you are part of—because you—you share the—the
    Somebodiness of me.

⧓   RUBY DEE   ⧓

Appreciation

you ask me what i want from you

well, i'll tell you

i want to be appreciated
i want you to acknowledge my specialness
i want my achievements
to be lined up in your memory

i want you to be overwhelmed sometimes
by my talents

i want you to feel in awe

i want you to applaud my successes
& celebrate my triumphs

i want you there with champagne for my victories
i want you there with a shoulder for my tears

i want you to realize that the time i have put/do put
into myself
is to make our relationship better

i want you to encourage my efforts
even if it means i surpass you!

i want you to take my seriousness, seriously
& respond accordingly

i want to be appreciated

for all the special, little things
that make me, me
i want to be appreciated

        ⋙   DOROTHY E. KING ⋘

I Want to Sing

i want to sing
a piercing note
lazily throwing my legs
across the moon
my voice carrying all the way
over to your pillow
    i want you

i need i swear to loll
about the sun
and have it smelt me
the ionosphere carrying
my ashes all
the way over
to your pillow
    i want you

 NIKKI GIOVANNI

Pulled Tightly

I need you! In this state of desire
    everything is pulled tightly
    like a bow.

Caress me with your voice. Move
    against the longing and
    release my arrow.

BERNARD V. FINNEY, JR.

Talking That Talk

I want to know you like orange sunrises in egypt
want to be with you like wind across clover-filled meadows
want to tell you like thunder rolling in the distance
want to keep you like rose buds unfolding

I want to hold you like a june sky holds a full moon
want to squeeze you like a stone grows from the earth
want to touch you like pink on satin
want to stroke you like fresh fallen snow

I want to fold you like the curve of a wave
want to spread you like the even hills of africa
want to spin you like a sandstorm in the desert

I want to dance you like a shooting star
want to sing you like cornfields in iowa
want to fly you like time goes after time
want to hone you like a crescent moon

I want to move you like still wind chimes
want to turn you like the curve of a peach
want to taste you like the first light of dawn
want to love you like a wheel going around, around and
around

DOUGHTRY LONG

A Love Poem

some things we take.
we need.
we give.

sometimes we take.
we care.
we love.

city full of people that
bloom like marigolds, lilac trees,
and african violets.
and for me,
some days,

there is only you and me.

and sometimes i give my love to you.
and sometimes,
i take.

CAROLYN M. RODGERS

That Kiss

that kiss was for you
but i gave it to him
because he's here
and you're not

and lately he's been getting a lot of things
that belong to you
like my tentative smile
and my quick laugh
and my sarcastic
but appropriate comments

and when my love needs to shower
he comes running with buckets
while if *you* come
it's with an umbrella
and rain attire

baby, i've got an enormous amount of love to give
and it's warm, special love
just for you

but i'm giving it to him
because i need to give
and you're distancing
and he's approaching

and if i really didn't care about you
would i be telling you this now?

DOROTHY E. KING

Marriage Counsel

Marriage counselor said to me,
"You know your Edgar loves you.
It happens with a man sometimes.
Okay! A few lost days now and then
But he'll be back again.
His heart is home with you!
Trust me!"
I said,
"I know home is where his *heart* is
But damn that!
I wanna be where the rest of him is at."

RUBY DEE

Moonbeams

The pale moonbeams carry us into
    a deeper place within our
    night.
    Somehow,
    Somehow,
        we find love in the
        coves and in the
        paleness.

Please do not leave me when my moods
    make me a burden to you. I
    need to be heard and to be
    loved. Stay next to me and
    give me what I have never had.

ELIZABETH I. ROBERTS

Seduction

Before the Act
(Dedicated to Women)

Before we become intimate
You must show me
That you really know
How to love me,
Spiritually.
You can show this love
With your smile,
Your touch, your gaze,
Your hushed words,
Your caring and sharing,
Your respect, trust
And loyal friendship.
Only then, and in due time,
And, after you have declared
Your God-given love for me
And I have declared mine for you,
Only then, can we truly,
truly love each other.

BARBARA-MARIE GREEN

!!!He!!!

He wanted to make love to me.
I wanted him to,
            but I stopped him.
There was nothing out there but him
                and me
                        and trees
                            and grass
                                and birds
                                    and . . . .
            . . . . him . . . .
He was tall and handsome and sure of himself.
                            I was small and scared.
His voice was soft,
            deep,
                reassuring,
                    loving.
                            Mine was shaking.
His eyes were kind
            and understanding.
                            My eyes were crying.
His touch was soft and gentle.
                    And I was scared to death.
He took complete control of me.
                    There was nothing I could say or do.
            I was scared.

He wanted to make love to me.
I wanted him to,
        but I stopped him.
                There was nothing . . . . . .

EMILY M. NEWSOME

Black Love in the Afternoon

Love in the afternoon, is wonderful,
        is terrific, is exciting
Love in the afternoon
        is a special delight
Love in the afternoon
        no rushing, no deadlines,
        no schedules, no business,
        no distractions
        no interruptions.
Love in the afternoon, is different,
        is soothing, is tender,
        sweet and sensual
Love in the afternoon
        is lunch, tennis
        swimming, massage
        beauty therapy
        and thoughtful
You have all the time
        in the world to explore
        to massage, to caress
        to experiment,
To enjoy and complete ecstasy of loving
in broad daylight
Love at night may come and go
But you will never, never forget
        LOVE IN THE AFTERNOON

      DENNIS RAHIIM WATSON

Seduction

one day
you gonna walk in this house
and i'm gonna have on a long African
gown
you'll sit down and say "The Black . . ."
and i'm gonna take one arm out
then you—not noticing me at all—will say "What about
this brother . . ."
and i'm going to be slipping it over my head
and you'll rapp on about "The revolution . . ."
while i rest your hand against my stomach
you'll go on—as you always do—saying
"I just can't dig . . ."
while i'm moving your hand up and down
and i'll be taking your dashiki off
then you'll say "What we really need . . ."
and i'll be licking your arm
and "The way I see it we ought to . . ."
and unbuckling your pants
"And what about the situation . . ."
and taking your shorts off
then you'll notice
your state of undress
and knowing you you'll just say
"Nikki,
isn't this counterrevolutionary . . . ?"

NIKKI GIOVANNI

Good to Be in You

Good to be in you.
Good, too, to be near you.
To feel your shoulder touching mine
and know that all night we shall lie side by side,
and in the morning
you will wake me with your gentle movements about the
    room.

Good to be in you.
God, too, to be with you.
To sit at table and look into your eyes
and see feelings, like wind over grass or water,
stir your sensitive face,
to exchange our families and our childhoods,
and know that our souls have kissed.

DUDLEY RANDALL

Autumn Poems

the heat
you left with me
last night
still smolders
the wind catches
your scent
and refreshes
my senses

i am a leaf
falling from your tree
upon which i was
impaled

NIKKI GIOVANNI

The Doorway That We Hide Behind

The doorway that we hide behind;
The dark alcove where emotions lie
And we,
          too afraid
                    too shy
to let our whispered thoughts be heard
Exchange a look, instead of words
          And quick
                    before we're caught
                    press close,
My body trembling against yours
          like a fresh cut rose,
          gasping for life
          and reaching honey
                    yellow
                    petals
          toward the warmth
                              of sun and light;
Perhaps
We might
          in time
Speak of this peculiar meeting
                    and let our minds
                    like lovers, touch;
          (There is no rush)
We may spend our lives alone

Inside these tenement, ghetto homes
                          growing old,
With never a private
                          moment of our own
To wish,
        or daydream,
                          or kiss;
That's why we cling like this;
        in the darkness;
Escaping from the bitter climb,
Coming,
At the same time.

⌵   DEE DEE MCNEIL   ⌵

Flowers

When you make love
to me
I must confess,
your eyes are
April, moist,
poetic.
With their lovely light,
they open my fingers
to catch the silence
of your sweet flesh.
Each time,
with each move,
we make a garden.

SYBIL KEIN

Please Disturb

I left your dinner
   in the oven to keep it warm
   'cause I know how you
dislike cold food.

I gave our son
   his nightly bath
   read him tall tales
'til he fell asleep.

I brushed my hair
   'til it shined like silver
   in the dark.
     And my teeth
     are the squeaky kind of clean
that sinks are
when cleaned with ajax.

I washed my body slowly,
   in white bubbles
   that smell of lilacs
     And by candlelight
     I soothed myself
with soft sweet powder.

I wrapped myself
   in your old blue shirt,
   purposely laid myself
   across the entire bed to say
"please disturb."

DOROTHY MEEKINS

One Nighter

The night our eyes met
    I did not see what lay
        beneath
The warmth and tenderness
    you brought to me that evening,

Oh Barbados, thank you
    for the happening—

I remember every moment
    the looks
        the touch
            the laughter.

But it was the passion
    that lifted my soul to
        its greatest heights—

And Yes that first caress
        that lingers on my lips
           till now.

I'd love to look into those
    eyes once more.

DARNLEY OSBORNE

Morning Thoughts

i want
to wake up
with you
beside me
let my kisses
be your alarm clock
hold up the day
while we say
good morning

i want
to roll
into your arms
watch the sun
streak your face
ask the birds
to perform
your favorite song

i want
to lie
quietly beside you
listen to the cadence
of your breathing
hang a
"do not disturb" sign
on the morning

i want
to wake up
with you
beside me
& then
i want
to make love

DOROTHY E. KING

Untitled

Let me come to you naked
come without my masks
come dark
       and lay beside you

Let me come to you old
come as a dying snail
come weak
       and lay beside you

Let me come to you angry
come shaking with hate
come callused
       and lay beside you

even more

Let me come to you strong
come sure and free
come powerful

and lay with you

PAT PARKER

"If I Go All the Way Without You Where Would I Go?"

(The Isley Brothers)

there/ to the right of venus
                        close to where yr lion
stalks our horizon/   see/
listen/
glow scarlet/ char-scarlet/ set my heart down
there/   near you/ scaldin *amarillo*/
oh/ say/ my new day
                        my dawn/
yr fingers trace the rush of my lips/
                        ever so reverent/
                                ever so hungry/

here/
to the right side of venus/
                        my tongue/
                        tropical lightenin/
rush/ now/ softly/ tween my toes/ the seas ebb
& in these sands/ i've come back/
                an unpredictable swell
a fresh water lily/ in the north atlantic/
when you touch me/   yes
that's how pearls somehow/ rip from the white of my
bones

to yr fingertips/
    incontrovertible hard chicago/
        rococo implications/
& this/   the mississippi delta/ tween my thighs
yr second touch/ forbids
a thing less/ than primordial fluidity/

no/
i lay next to you/
    the undertow at carmel/
the russian river/ feelin up stalks of the best/ of
humboldt county
& damn it/
    what makes you think/ my spine is
yr personal/
san andreas fault?

        shiftin/ serene fields break for rain/
til
i open/ deep brown moist & black
    cobalt sparklin everywhere/
we are
there/
    where the pacific fondles my furthest
shores/ detroit-high-russet/ near redwoods/
    i am climbin
        you chase me/ from limb to limb/
        pullin/ the colored stars/ out the
night
        slippin em/ over my tongue/
&
i thought i cd get over/
the dangers/ of livin
    on the pacific rim/
when i look at you/
i

know/ i am riskin my life/
    tossin reason/ to the outback of the far
rockaways/
             goin/ givin up/ everything/ with out
protest/

givin up/ meteorological episodes
the appalachian mountains/
           handin over/ islands from puget
sound/
        travis county hill country/
givin away/ treasures/
i
never
claimed/
    til i felt you/

my own december sunset/ teasin cypress/
even campbell street bikers/ in downtown oakland/
i stopped resistin/
what won't/ be orderly/ imagined/ legitimate/
yes/ yes/
hold me
like/ the night grabs wyoming/
& i am more/ than i am not/
i cd sing sacred lyrics/ to songs i don't know/
my cheek/ rubs gainst the nappy black/ cacti of yr
chest/
& i am a flood/ of supernovas/
if you kiss me like that/ i'm browned wetlands
yr lips/ invite the moon/ to meander/
our mouths open & sing/
yes/
our tongues/
the edge of the earth/

Ntozake Shange

99

Perfumed Moments with My Man

Perfumed moments
sachet
through my mind.
You
sniff me.
Whiff me.
Lick me.
Prick me.
Stick me
like a corsage on your chest.
Flower me.
Shower me.
Deliciously deliver me.
Quiver me
with your sweet smelling
pumpkin pie and cinnamon
October kiss.
Chocolate never tasted like this!

Plant your passion fruit.
Fill my bowl.
Banana sweet,
coconut hard.
Slippery as lard.
Slide me.
Ride me.

Hide me
beneath the cover
of your cologne.
Expose everything I own.

Hose my rose garden.
Suckle my vine.
Read my mind.
Fire me up.
Wire me up.
Ground me.
Pound me.
Lay me soundly
asleep
in the orange blossom bosom of your deep;
of your dark.
Play your harp.
Blow me.
Show me
every jasmine song you learned to sing.
Turn sterile winter
into cherry blossom spring.

Dip me.
Flip me.
Dew me
with the nectar that you spray.
Taste my sweet bouquet.
Pollinate my day.
Inhale me.
De-rail me.
Ride me like a train.
Remember when I came
time and time again?
Quick as a hummingbird,
Rowdy as a hawk.
Dancing like the Jabber-Walk!

Sing!!
Spread my wings.
Fly me.
Tie me.
Toss me
like petals down the aisle.
Oil me.
Spoil me
in the hothouse of your smile.
Orchid whispers blush my cheeks.
Sweep me off my feet.
Lift me.
Swiftly
Kiss me.
Take my breath away.
Make me beg for you to stay.

Hug me.
Tug me.
Twist my feelings into gold.
Ring my fingers
Touch my soul.
Smell me.
Tell me
Irrevocable you care.
Place your stem
right through the rose buds
in my hair.
Arrange me.
Don't change me.
Put my feelings in a vase.
Delicate and sensitive
like kisses on your face.

Caress me.
Undress me.
Pat and press me
like flowers in a book.
Keep me
discreetly.
Only you
complete me.
Only you can
touch me
with a look.

DEE DEE MCNEIL

My Tongue Paints a Path

My tongue paints a path of fire
Across her body
My tongue trickles unseen
And indelible tracks
Through the center of her metropolis—
As a flameless torch,
I burn beyond the color
Of heat into infinite fire:
Where her passion
Is one long sigh of molten air
That my tongue
Banks to a burnsong:
Against the anvil of her geography:
That my tongue *rings*—
Where my tongue plunges plunges
Into the waters of her country—
Into the ravines,
The crops,
Of her forests.

EUGENE REDMOND

Quietly

I woke up this morning,
Looked at you sleeping next to me.
In the bathroom the electric light
Cut between me and my mirrored image.
I relieved myself, showered
And as I washed, I thought: of last night,
Of our struggling in the grip of love,
Of our winning the struggle,
Of our relaxing
Triumphant.
Immediately, I rinsed the soap away,
Returned to bed
And touched you,
Quietly.

HERBERT WOODWARD MARTIN

Revelations

New Face

I have learned not to worry about love;
but to honor its coming
with all my heart.
To examine the dark mysteries
of the blood
with headless heed and
swirl,
to know the rush of feelings
swift and flowing
as water.
The source appears to be
some inexhaustible
spring
within our twin and triple
selves;
the new face I turn up
to you
no one else on earth
has ever
seen.

ALICE WALKER

His Shirt

does not show his
true colors. Ice-

blue and of stuff
so common

anyone
could have bought it,

his shirt
is known only

to me, and only
at certain times

of the day.
At dawn

it is a flag
in the middle

of a square
waiting to catch

chill light.
Unbuttoned, it's

a sail surprised
by boundless joy.

In candlelight at turns
a penitent's

scarf or beggar's
fleece, his shirt is

inapproachable.
It is the very shape

and tint
of desire

and could be mistaken
for something quite

fragile and
ordinary.

≫ RITA DOVE ≪

I Just Couldn't

I wanted to tell the whole world
About my love for you
But I just couldn't.
I wanted to dance my love
Sing it or write a poem
But I just couldn't.
I dreamed a fantastic dream
Of me in your arms
And a long warm kiss.
I wanted the cat to answer me back
When I held her and called your name.
But she just couldn't.
I tried to tell my little sister
About my love for you
So that her big eyes could look at me
The way I want you to
But she was asleep and so
I just couldn't.
My folks say I'm too young
To be falling in love.
I tried to change my heart
To make my mind stop thinking
About you so much.
But I just couldn't.

I wrote your name on all the pages
of my diary.
I took a letter I wrote you
To the mailbox—
But I just couldn't.

HASNA MUHAMMAD

A Quarter for Your Thoughts

Might as well tell you

I love you

It's not as deep as the ocean or
wide as the sea
just a little love

Little like a toddler's steps
    mild like the taste of a favorite dish
        served the next day

I love you
easy as pie
simple as that.

JALEELAH KARRIEM

Revelation

Turn sideways now and let them see
What loveliness escapes the schools,
Then turn again, and smile, and be
The perfect answer to those fools
Who always prate of Greece and Rome,
"The face that launched a thousand
   ships,"
And such like things, but keep tight lips
For burnished beauty nearer home.
Turn in the sun, my love, my love!
What palm-like grace! What poise! I
   swear
I prize these dusky limbs above
My life. What laughing eyes! What
   gleaming hair!

HILTON A. VAUGHAN

I'm Beginning to See Lights . . .

(from a male chauvinist)

I'm beginning to see lights
Click on in your big, beautiful
                              Eyes
Our love is too solid to break up
Over minor things
Like who washes the pots and pans
After your tuna casserole
You like to plow through dirt
I like to step around it
Avoiding all contact

While you, I think, are
Beginning to recognize
We each have certain strengths
Which complement!
That our virtues should be joined
Into an even more perfect union
                              And Yes

I saw lights
Click on in your big, beautiful
                              Eyes
When I smiled and said:
"I'll wash the pots and pans
after you make your wonderful
tuna casserole."

LINDSAY PATTERSON

Young Tender

Although the years separate
        us
And our views and ideas
        are not in sync,
I find that time spent
        away from you
Has no meaning.

The body that once showed
        form and proportion
Has given way to bumps
        here and there.
Perhaps it's through your
        presence
I live and try to rekindle
        My youth.

I have done many things
        before you
Toured the world, read many
        books and loved.
But let not these experiences
        frighten you
I'm prepared to do it all
        again with you
For the first time.

DARNLEY OSBORNE

Serial Monogamy

i think/ we should reexamine/ serial monogamy
is it/ one at a time or
one for a long time?
>   how
does the concept of infinity relate to a skilled
serial monogamist/ & can
that person consider a diversionary escapade
a serial
one night stand?
>   can a consistent
serial monogamist
have one/ several/ or myriad relationships
that broach every pore of one's body
>   so long as there is no penetration?
do we/ consider adventurous relentless tongues
capable of penetration & if we do
can said tongues whip thru us indiscriminately
with words/ like

>   "hello"
>   "oh, you lookin good"
>   "you jigglin, baby"
cd these be reckless immature violations of
serial monogamy?

i mean/
if my eyes light up cuz
   some stranger just lets go/ caint stop hisself
from sayin
           "yr name must be paradise"
    if i was to grin or tingle/ even get a lil happy/
    hearin me & paradise/ now synonyms
does that make me a scarlet woman?
     if i wear a red dress that makes someone else hot
     does that put me out of the fryin pan & into the
fire?

say/
my jade bracelet got hot
              (which aint possible cuz jade aint
jade
          if it aint cold)
but say
my jade got lit up & burst offa my wrist
& i say/
     "i gotta find my precious stones
cuz they my luck"
         & he say
"luck don't leave it goes where
you need it"
       & i say
"i gotta find my bracelet"
       & he say
"you know for actual truth
           you was wearing this bracelet?"
& i say
  "a course, it's my luck"
       & he say
"how you know?"

& i say
   "cuz
   i heard my jade
   flyin thru the air
   over yr head
   behind my knees
   &
   up under the Japanese lampshade!"
      & he say
"you heard yr jade flyin thru the air?"
      "yes"
         i say
"& where were they flyin from"
      he say
   "from my arm" i say
   "they got hot & jumped offa my arm"
"but/
where was yr arm?"
         he say
& i caint say mucha nothin
cuz
where my arm was a part a some tremendous
current/
cd be 'lectricity or niggahs on fire/
so where my arm was is where/ jade gets hot
& does that imply the failure of serial monogamy?

do flamin flyin jade stones
on a arm/ that is a kiss/ & a man who knows where/
luck is
take the serial/ outta monogamy/ & leave
love?

      ⛌ NTOZAKE SHANGE ⛌

Secret Life

(for Zaron)

we have a secret life,
you and i.
a life between the darkness
and the light
with your mouth on my,
my mouth on your . . .

we have a secret life
that binds us
and blinds us
and finds us gasping
and giggling
and grasping
at a way to stop time.

we have a secret life,
a movie in my mind
that flashes when they ask me
what i see in you.
what can i do?
how can i tell them
it's your mouth on my,
my mouth on your . . .

so i don't even try.
i know the strength of secrets
is only in their keeping
and the beauty of the love
is always in the seeking
of that moment nothing matters
but that moment nothing matters.

we have a secret life,
a life between
the darkness and the light,
that keeps the world at bay
and makes it all alright.

PEARL CLEAGE

Can You?

i have to hand
it to you—

your lovemaking is great.
you know a thousand positions
                    movements
                    words
                    kisses
                    caresses
which make the good
better than ever
                    seemed possible;
but as you take
my body's fingertips
and we scale that
                    mountain
to its greatest height—
    —its highest peak—
you know we must
come down,
descend once again
to the
            plains below
where there is just
                    the you of you
                    and me of me

devoid temporarily
of sexual desires
                 and things of that
sort to hinge
   our relationship on.

can you touch my mind—
             —my soul—
as skillfully
          in the plain
as you have touched
        my body
               in the mountain?

≳   LINDA COUSINS ≴

For the Men Who Ask:
Will You Write a Poem for Me?

it is hard for her to know which part
of them is doing the asking:
is it the slice of small boy wedged within the man
hungrily yearning for maternal crusts of love,
the warm and steamy stuff made from scratch,
and tenderly shaped just for them, from womanly dough?
or is it the portion of masculine gingerbread-ego
in need of leavening, and puffy hunks of self-importance
that is doing the asking?

it is her feminine center that intuitively suspects
there is an instinctively lustful piece of them
longing to drink the heady sweetness of blackberry ink,
taste the meat and muscle of the written word,
and the sundry power of her particular pen,
the whimsical hope of sapping some of her substance
and possessing it, as if it were their very own.

they will come to know, it takes an extraordinary man
to eat from her poetic plate, drink from her cup of ink:
it is by invitation only, and usually she dines alone.

BEVERLEY WIGGINS WELLS

Loving Too Much

I Loved you much too much
Much more than I should have
As I look back, no man should ever again,
Give love on earth the way I gave love to you

Emptied my body, mind and spirit
Opened the vault, withdrew all funds from the heart,
Manufactured new love in my brain
Borrowed love on credit from God

I loved you much too much too much,
No one should ever get to a point where
they do not have one drop of love left for themselves.

DENNIS RAHIIM WATSON

Long Glances

If I looked
long glances at you
what would you do?
Would you look back, or away,
intending to convey you've noticed
nothing at all

If my eyes
stroked your cheek would you
stiffen your spine
and frown or, to be polite,
smile, so that I might
not feel small?

If I, with a look,
were to signal how
I think of you
what would you think of me?
One day I must look
long glances at you and see.
One day . . . soon.

MICKI GRANT

Be Warned

ALTHOUGH
YOU DO NOT LOVE
ME YET
EMOTION HAS
A STRANGE WAY OF
ENTERING THE
NERVOUS SYSTEM
AND CLUTCHING
THE HEART . . .
NOT VICIOUSLY
YOU UNDERSTAND
BUT VIOLENTLY.

LINDSAY PATTERSON

Reflections on Lost Love

End Notes

if parting is necessary
part as lovers.
part as two people
who can still
smile & talk & share
the good & important
with each other.
part
wishing the other
happy
happy life
in a world
fighting against the
beautiful,
fighting against the
men & women,
sisters and brothers
Black as
we.

HAKI MADHUBUTI/DON L. LEE

For the Count

Bring out the crystal glasses
one for you
and one for me
and as you pour the wine
I will reflect on the time gone by
and the love between us then that is no more
I will try to leave
more
silently
than I came

call in the spirits to join us in this
our last night
our last drink
together
a tribute, final, to the way we were last week
and the week before,
tell them to dress in bright colors
and then you tell me,
"How shall I toast you"
Should I say,
"to love, to life, to us?"

Light the candles,
let the humming and the chanting begin
let us dance in a circle

and when it has been broken
let there be only smiles for what we had

say that I appeared in your life
because
someone wished it
and you are not to blame
and I will
more than likely
say the same

᠉ MAE JACKSON ᠉

CJ–The End

go forth

knowing

that i love you

that i wish only good things
for you

that i hope you find your rainbow
with a golden pot
full of whatever it is you desire

that while our time together was brief
it filled a lifetime worth of dreams

go forth
with the tender feelings
i tear from my heart
to share with you

go forth
knowing
that i will remember it all
every moment

Dorothy E. King

The Lie

Today, you threaten to leave me.
I hold curses, in my mouth,
which could flood your path, sear
bottomless chasms in your road.

I keep, behind my lips,
invectives capable of tearing
the septum from your
nostrils and the skin from your back.

Tears, copious as a spring rain,
are checked in ducts
and screams are crowded in a corner
of my throat.

You are leaving?

Aloud, I say:
I'll help you pack, but it's getting late,
I have to hurry or miss my date.
When I return, I know you'll be gone.
Do drop a line or telephone.

MAYA ANGELOU

Last Poem I'm Gonna Write Bout Us

some
      times i dream bout
                  u & me
                        runnen down
a street laughen.
           me no older
           u no younger
                than we be.
& we finalee catch
           each other.
                laugh.   tooouch
in the nite.
           some
              times
                i turn a corner
of my mind
        & u be there
                loooooking
                    at me.
& smilen.
        yo/far/away/smile.
               & i moooove
to u.
     & the day is not any day.   & yes ter day
is looonNNg
           goooNNe. & we just be. Some

times i be steady dreamen bout u

                            cuz i waaannNt
neeeeEEeeD   u   so
            baaaAdDD.
        with u no younger &
        me no older
               than we be.

        ⬙   SONIA SANCHEZ ⬙

Reaching Back

I keep reaching back for the magic of those first few days
    when we found each other.
When we discovered that we both liked mayonnaise on
    hamburgers medium well done,
And neither had ever read *Wuthering Heights*.
When we concurred on the agonies of war and disagreed
    about the importance of being earnest.

When your touch was gentle, and your eyes bright
As you told me about taking over new york city before it
    overtook you.
When you ran your fingers softly through my hair,
Asking if it was all right to mess it up
And needing no answer.
When I made you laugh,
And your laughing made me feel good.

I keep reaching back for that exact moment when you
    reached for me
And I came into your arms for our first kiss—
Hesitant, unsure, afraid to be too eager,
Very happy to be there.

This fairy tale gone bad,
This sweet spring fruit withered before ripening—

Is it that the flower blossoms too quickly, and therefore
    closes too soon?

Or are we too strongly molded in our separate worlds?

I keep reaching back, reaching back for the magic of those
    first days when we found each other.

I keep reaching back,
                    and grasping—

                            nothing.

       SAUNDRA SHARP

Freedom

I have learned your ways.
I have learned the mellow
              sweetness of your laughter.
                        I have heard your
              deep bass voice,
       calm and clear,
vibrating through the church on a snowy Sunday morning
   in December.
I have seen warmth,
       concern,
          sorrow,
            and yes,
               even love in your hazel eyes.
I have felt the gentle strength of your warm embrace.
                    I have known
            the tenderness
      of your kisses.
I now know the reasoning behind
          some of the things you did
                that I did not
           then
       understand.
But, I see something in your eyes.
        Something different in your mannerism.
        What are you saying . . . . . . ?
Well, I've been expecting it for quite some time now,

And I am sorry that it could not have lasted longer.
But it's over now,
       and I grant you
            your
               freedom.

Emily M. Newsome

Somewhere in the City

You are somewhere in the city, lost to me,
But sharing buildings, skyline, traffic signals,
Street names, rush hours, and street scenes;
Sharing unconsciously the things we do not share
By purpose anymore.
And though we do not meet, and though our feet
Do not strike the same pavement at the same time,
You are mine as the city is mine.
You and the city are one.
The city cannot enclose me in its foggy arms
Without your arms, too, holding me in a loose embrace.

Somewhere in the city you are driving someone somewhere
Or telephoning, or taking a bath,
Or making love, or watching a movie, or working,
Or polishing the metal on the car you are so proud of,
Or getting sleepy over wine,
Or telling jokes, or playing a jukebox in a bar.

How many times have I barely missed you
By one block or one door or a one-way street?

Somewhere you are forgetting me
And making of me nothing—
No more than the song you listen to

Or the joke you tell—
Not so much, really!

My eyes will be impassable as fog
If we should ever meet again,
As bright as street lights,
As shallow as rain, as hard as steel.
The soft soul-eyes you knew will be for you
The barren city,
The city without love or hope or mercy or desire.
Without remembrances, without nostalgia,
Without soul.
And you will not realize or understand
How often I caress you
When the downtown lights blink on
And the traffic signals change from red to green.

⊲⊲ NAOMI LONG MADGETT ⊳⊳

Souvenirs

my love has left me has gone from me
   and I with no keepsake nothing
   not a glove handkerchief lock of hair picture
   only in memory

the first night the magic snowfall
   the warm blue-walled room we looking out at the snow
   listening to music drinking the same cocktail
   she pressing my hand searching my eyes
   the first kiss my hands touching her
   she close to me answering my lips
   waking at morning eyes opening slowly

I approaching her house trembling
   kissing her entering the room
   waking all night writing a poem for her
   thinking of her planning her pleasure
   remembering her least liking and desire
   she cooking for me eating with me
   kissing me with little kisses over the face
   we telling our lives till morning

   more to remember better to forget
   she denying me slashing my love
   all pain forgotten if only she comes back to me

        ▓▓   DUDLEY RANDALL ▓▓

Jazzy Vanity

She was really neat, man.
Great mind . . . bearing . . . purpose.
I felt something was missing,
Wasn't sure what or where in her the thing was Loose.
Ran my spirit all through her.
Couldn't find it!
Air, beauty and mind, brother, that was all. Tough!
What a shame. A mellow lady. Out of sight. Really together,
    baby.
But, had to cut her loose! Something was missing. She wasn't
    wrapped up
Tight enough.
Where was it?
I wonder could it have slipped through that crack
In my jar!

RICHARD W. THOMAS

Reflections on a Lost Love

*(for my brothers who think they are lovers
and my sisters who are the real-lovers)*

back in chi/
all the blackwomen
are fine,
super fine.
even the ones who:
    dee bob/ de bop/ she-shoo-bop
    bop de-bop/ dee dee bop/ dee-she dee-she-bop
    we—We eeeeeeeeee eeeee/ WEEEEEEE EEEEEEEE
they so fine/
that
when i slide up
to one & say: take it off   sing
               take it off   slow
                  take it all off   with feeling

& she would say: "if i doos,
            does u think u can groove dad——dy"
& i wd say: "can chitlins smell,
        is toejam black,
        can a poet, poet,
        can a musician, music?"

weeeee/ weeeeeee/ de-bop-a-dee-bop
whooo-bop/ dee-bop a-she-bop
as she smiled
& unbuttoned that top button
i sd: take it off sing
take it off slow
take it all off with feeling
first the skirt,
then the blouse
& next her wig (looked like she made it herself)
next the shoes & then
the eyelashes and jewelry
&
dee-bop/ bop-a-ree-bop/ WOW
the slip
& next the bra (they weren't big, but that didn't scare me)
cause i was grooven now: dee/ dee-bop-a-she-bop/
weeeeeEEEEEEEEEE
as she moved to the most important part,
i got up & started to groove myself but my eyes stopped
me.
first
her stockens down those shapely legs—
followed by black bikini panties, that just slid down
and
i just stood—
& looked with utter amazement as she said: in a deep
"hi baby—my name is man-like
joe sam." voice

HAKI MADHUBUTI/DON L. LEE

Why?

I wonder why she didn't
    call before leaving?

She promised she would—

I wonder why the letter
    never arrived?

Perhaps the Jamaican sun
    dulls the senses.

I wonder why she didn't
    know
That snow-filled nights alone
    would only make me miss her
      more.

I wonder why she broke
    her promise

I wonder why I wonder—

DARNLEY OSBORNE

For Your Information B.W.

You are in love.
You can see what others
cannot see, the wind:
It is a green incandescent
mass dotted with little
silver bells that tinkle
and sometimes howl.

You can touch what others
cannot touch, the sky:
It is brittle like spun
glass and warms the hands.

You can hear what others
cannot hear, snowflakes:
They have the sound of
ghosts break dancing on a
newly tinned roof.

Yet you cannot feel what
it is you would like to
feel, because you cannot
see or hear or touch what-
ever it is that pains you—
Me?

LINDSAY PATTERSON

Love Equation

math was simple then.

you plus me equalled one.

with you, i became whole.

i understood the meaning
of yin and yang,
cause and effect,
earth and sky.

don't good things come in pairs?

then you left.

just when i thought i had
it all figured out. now
two minus one equals

nothing.

no matter how many
times i subtract.

HAZEL CLAYTON HARRISON

Starting Over

He said he wanted to start anew.

"It's time to start over now,
the two of you slow me
down," he said.

"From What," I asked.

Running a race with life and his wife and son slowed him
down.
He could move faster and do a lot more,
alone.

"But you love *me*," I said.

He packed hurriedly, and continued,
"I love you, but I'm *not* in love *with* you.
You're a word's person, I'm a number's person.
She knows me better than you do already.
We have different goals, you and I.
I want power,
you're satisfied with what you have."

All the while, I was standing there, sinking into a state of
depression and wondering what it all meant.

"And anyway," I yelled, "who could possibly know you better than I.
I've loved you. I bore your son. I've read between your lines and in-between your lines for more than ten years."

He grabbed the Sentinel, a drawing he had given me as a birthday present.

"You can't take the Sentinel, it was a present. Things were good with us then, leave it alone. It belongs to me," I cried.

He retreated and laid it down.

As I grabbed the Sentinel and clutched it for dear life, I sobbed and stated, "Power, but power, how much more power can you get, than to save a black boy's life."

He left anyway.

⌘ DOROTHY MEEKINS ⌘

Mountain Suite in Winter

I. A Road Painting

> I blow through the tunnel
> At Lehigh with lights blaring
> And pop into daylight
> Like new birth
> Amazed by the sobriety
> Of winter birds
> Lifting like dark shadows
> For an instant
> Then dropping lightly
> To ground,
> Covered by snow.

II. Rain

> The smell is mountain laurel
> Faint beyond measure
> As we drive into hills
> Only seen on windless days
> and fair.
>
> Rounding the last bend
> You gesture to the lake at sunset,
> Touch my moist fingers on the wheel.

You commence a song
that will not cease until
the loons cry,
Brilliant,
At the break of day.

III. When I Knew You Were Leaving

That evening,
the land worked the water's edge.
The moon was white in a sky of unbroken blue.
The lake's foil glimmered like metal at
sunset.
Moving clouds became mountains as the sun
fell.

I thought of mid-western waters
And you beside them on this holiday,
One year hence:
Your touch an impossibility,
Your mouth a smile for
Men I shall never meet,
Your flesh cool
Beyond my power to
Warm it,
Or bring back this moment
(even in exact memory)
When you are still,
A possible lover.

⬚ HOUSTON A. BAKER, JR. ⬚

Your Place

There is a place in my heart where you will always live.
A place where the sound of your laughter when your spirit has
been touched will resound.
A place where the warmth of your eyes melts the doubts of
my spirit and heals the brokenness that the world,
and you,
put there.
A place where your hands will always minister to me in a way
that no one else's ever will, and your smile will give me
nourishment that nothing else can provide.
A place where dreams of our tomorrows flourish and prosper.
It is a place that used to occupy my whole heart.
It grows smaller with every passing day that you
choose not to understand.
It may one day
disappear altogether,
but that depends on how much of my heart I can give away in
some other direction . . .
and,
if you ever come to understand.
Whatever happens,
I will always carry the reality of you,
at least in some
small
place in my heart.

EMILY M. NEWSOME

A Place Called Comfort

The last time I gave my lover a bath, my hands caressed his smooth black skin. The small ripples of waves brushed gently against the tub, taking with them lifeless skin, that retreated to the foot of the tub.

The essence of flowers added sweet smells and candlelight danced against the walls. I stroked him gently and wished the night could last forever. His perfectly chiseled body lay limp from the steam created by the hot water and his eyelids relaxed to a near closed position.

Sometimes now, as I fall asleep, I remember that time, the pleasant small talk and my escalating emotions. He melted inside me that day and I found within the experience, a place called Comfort.

The last time I gave my lover a bath, I went to a place that protected me from all the pain that my life has known, a place called Comfort.

DOROTHY MEEKINS

Old Love

how strange—
to meet a memory from your past,
someone, you thought you knew but didn't. to
feel as if your makeup, your lipstick, your
skirt needs adjusting,
along with your heartbeat, your breathing, and
your soul.

CAROLYN M. RODGERS

SECTION 8

Forever

Reaching

i
would
touch
you
f o r e v e r
if my arms
could
reach
that
far

DOROTHY E. KING

Time, Time,

This is my time
This is your time
This is our time together
Time - Time
Creeping out from the rocks of ages
The seas, sun, moon, rain, green leaves
From nothing
From everything that ever was
From microbe time to
Flesh and bones and blood time
Countless invisible tentacles
Making me distinct, separate
And just like you and
Especially like you
Your face a privilege
Your touch a recording
Your deaths all mine
In glory or despair
Part of the pattern—the dizzying pattern
That keeps on trying to improve itself
Throughout your—my time
Time—the traveler—snatching
Snatching at forever—searching
Searching for the unraveler
That perfects the pattern.
MEAN TIME

To laugh, to give, to cry
And try, try, try to
Reach out on this special ride.
To shout—shout
I want to love you—you
You—I love you
This The Trip
This is my time.
This is your time your
Time is my time. Our
Time together time time
The always today time time
The always now time
That gives eternity its dimension
That sparks everlasting's come
Come and find me come
Come and take me fire.

⧉   RUBY DEE   ⧉

Love Tight

PLACE YOUR HAND
INTO MY HAND AND

OPEN YOUR MOUTH
WIDE AS MY MOUTH

AND CLOSE YOUR EYES
AS TIGHT AS YOU CAN

THEN IMAGINE WE
BOTH ARE TWO

LIONS IN LOVE
FOREVER

TED JOANS

Treating My Lady Right

Every other morning . . .
I wake up early and serve my lady
breakfast in bed
And if she's running late for work,
I iron her blouse or dress

Throughout the week
I do her feet and nails.
On Fridays it's dinner and Broadway.
Because she's such a wonderful and
special friend, hang partner, advisor
and supporter, I surprise her with
bouquets of flowers, gifts and
plenty of loving.

I enjoy shopping for her clothes
I help her with the housework, homework
and career
On Saturday I do our laundry
If she's out jogging
I run her bubble bath . . .
and massage her tired body
with my finest oils

Because I don't like to fuss or fight . . .
I make it my business
to treat my lady right . . .
So she won't replace me overnight!

DENNIS RAHIIM WATSON

Untitled

it does not matter
how long you stay
forever
is in me
     and i control it.

your beauty
your joy
are mine
to recall
     always
     whenever . . .

your tenderness
is tucked around
the corners
of my heart
     matters not
     if we are
     together
     or apart

your gentleness
wakes me
with a smile
remembering

all those times
you held me tight
all through the night
remembering . . .

no
it does not matter
how long you stay
i keep you inside me
    in my
    very own
    special
    way

the glow
in your eyes
warms my soul
even after you've gone
to where
whom
or what
the glow
lingers
    and warms
    and warms
    and warms

✹ C. TILLERY BANKS ✹

Love Being Loved

i have loved
   being embraced
by man
         but there is no embrace
like the enduring
       and gentle
yet freeing embrace
            of the Spirit

i have loved
making love
to man
         but there is no love made
like the love
       of the Spirit
remaining ever
as One
with you

not separating
after moments of ecstasies
to become duality
once more

ever as one
       ever as One

in the loving
            embrace
in the climactic
                    high
of an inner life
that sustains
and remains
            eternally

and I need such
            sustaining
            and eternally
                        remaining
                                don't you?

ever as one
            ever as One
in the eternal
        sweet
        Love embrace

of the Spirit.

Now and Here After

When was our first meeting?
Forty-years? No, forty-five.
Years are poor compilers for our union
Our love distorts them—
Contracting and expanding time.

Was it chance
Or were we like the universe,
Being pulled by a great attractor?
If we were not at a particular place at an exact time,
Would our love have ever known each other?

Strangers look at our youthful photos:
Is that you or your children?
A grandchild smiles.
Where did our children go?

Are we just two again?
Visits and phone calls say *no*.
Yet, occasionally,
Our vision is unobstructed by loving bodies,
We view ourselves again.

I see you have defeated time.
No, built on it!
You tell me I'm the same.

Why can't I find a deceptive mirror,
That practices your love?

Youthful passion satisfied,
Love resides in the quietness of a glance
And the gentleness of a touch.
Wordless moments are shared thoughts.
To know you is to know myself
To know love is to know you.

ALLISON WEST

Senior Love

Easier to be hijacked on a plane
Than for a woman over sixty
To find a new love and marriage,
Some say.
But one woman beat the odds.
Her finding game was easy,
As a man and she . . .
Well, they found each other.
They dated a while, became good friends,
Then said, "I do," in church
Where at the altar they promised forever,
To love, honor and cling together
Though the odds be one in a million.

BARBARA-MARIE GREEN

SECTION 9

Letters of Love and Passion

Love Letter

Dearest Rogue,

Your plane had no sooner lifted off than I realized that something was missing—other than your fabulous self. I had been, in a word, robbed! Deftly, artfully, but robbed, nonetheless.

Admittedly, the rare stimulation of prolonged, spirited and intelligent conversation left me vulnerable. Is it any wonder then that, having been made giddy from the champagne of your lips and sedated under the gentle authority of your inquisitive fingers, I was rendered defenseless. The seduction complete, you calmly appropriated my heart and boarded your American Airlines flight westward, leaving me, smiling and waving in a euphoric stupor.

Well, my darling thief, now that I am no longer stupored, and my euphoria has been reduced to a bottomless pit of longing, your scheduled visit two months hence seems a lifetime away and is no longer acceptable. However, should your conscience be sufficiently pricked by this missive, prompting you to return quickly with the pilfered property, I am predisposed to be forgiving—even generous. I will happily make you a gift of the heart you now hold, on the condition that you leave your own in its stead.

Until your eagerly anticipated arrival, I remain

Your heart(less) victim.

(MICKI GRANT)

Letter to My Overseas Lover

Dear Lover,

Wear it lightly, this unnamed treasure that we found waiting and created together. Wrap it around you on days when your souls touch the ground, on days when your heart feels the draft and not the wind, on nights when silence is not a friend. On nights when you would cry to hear a balafon sing.

Tuck all of it—this sweetness, this soft moist mystery, into a place/space. And when you need it, wear it lightly and smile. Smile for us.

                                    Love,
                                    Saundra (Sharp)

Love Letter #67

1

Because of you I do not
sleep at night, my
soul a hostage to love's
insomnia: somehow the

realization that I must rise
at a certain hour each
morning escapes me, that I must
work to pay my bills.

2

I was late again this morning.
the boss stared with
disgust and rolled his eyes
as though there were no

hope. others frowned, some
sneered. but one lady,
older, with red lips, smiled,
and knew my fate.

CARL COOK

Love Letter:
Dreaming and Thanks for the Loving

A perfect stranger
stopped me
on the street
Said he snifted
my aroma
around the corner,
Tasted my dark, dark amber
in his pores
Eased the tall, svelte body
as I walked.
Rubbed the ripples
on my head
        Then he spoke.
PUBLICLY,
and whispered

I dreamed of you
    before we met.

Later,
My sisters asked me
was he black or white?
        I smiled
Look at me.

Black as Africa
Nappy as night.
          I simmered
100% juicy
the last blackberry
of the vine.

Dear Bill,

Thanks for the little laminated purse-size card that says, "how often I dreamed of you . . . before you came true." It touched me deeply. The thought that someone walked around the world longing to meet (I should say) bump into and love a black woman—dark, deep dark; bright, sharp minded; many textured; hair that feels rough against the skin.

I now know you mean it when you say I don't have to be blue-eyed with blond hair or even try to be, because in your dreams you dreamed of a woman—just like me.

You are very special to me now. I look forward to being everything you dreamed of—and to being loved, as is. Feeling me, as is, I will give you what you dreamed of—and much more.

See you soon.

                        Love,
                PEARL (DUNCAN)

Letter: Father to Son

November 23, 1994

To My Son, Darrell, On His Thirty-First Birthday,

Today, on your thirty-first birthday, is the age I was when you were born. Your birth was one of the happiest days in my life. As they say in sports, you were an impact player. You irreversibly altered our family's life for the better. As with the birth of your sister, Tracey, I learned again what a selfish person I was. To release the love that was stored up in me, I required my child's birth. Like most fathers when their sons are born, it's their rebirth. I exposed you to my concerns, enjoyments and loves while trying not to unduly influence you. Since we now have so much in common, I'm grateful for my failure and self-deception.

There are so many happy experiences and moments that you have given me that it would take another lifetime to list them. Your bedtime musings, when you were about nine, still warmly touch my heart. You would call out to me at nights from your bedroom, "Daddy, come here! I got something to ask you!" The question that still brings a smile was when you asked, "Why do we have bones?" I attempted to explain how bones function, and you interrupted, "I know what they do, but why do we have them?" Then, you became godly as you reconstructed the human anatomy. In your view, there were certainly other materials better than bones that could do the same job without the risk of breaking. I also know there is a question that you are still asking: "What do people want out of life?" We discussed fame, fortune and all that glittered. In the end, I told you that you would have to search for that answer yourself. All I could do was to expose you to what I *considered useful* in your search. If nothing else, you know you are an extension of your parents' love and judgement.

The major differences between us when I was your age are that you are single and without children. Although you are far better prepared than I was to make a living, you don't have the wealth of an infant like yourself to damper your musings and lovingly refocus your priorities. Life is still mostly your viewpoint, and I know at times that singular view can be a lonely view. You've reminded me over the years that I told you that you would learn to know your loves and dislikes and have the privilege to search for your wants. And it was your responsibility to make an honest effort to develop and use your abilities. Your young life has reflected those tenets. I never told you that I am very proud of you—not because of your accomplishments, but because of who you are. I see a young man, who has now become a true friend, performing to his capabilities in a very competitive world, still honestly searching for his bliss, and most importantly, his capacity for love is growing.

So on your thirty-first birthday, I wish for you what you gave me when I was your age: love, courage, and a sense of proportion to search for my heart's desires.

HAPPY BIRTHDAY, SON!

Love,
DAD (ALLISON WEST)

Letter: Father to Daughter

December 23, 1994

Dear Tracey,

I haven't had an opportunity to talk to you since this lovable despot came into the family. His whimpers are our commands. All I can do is watch you care for him and listen to you lecture your mother and me on baby-sitting for our grandchild. I won't test your love and tell you what we say about you after you are out of ear reach.

The more I see your child, the more I see my daughter, and a kaleidoscope of colorful memories, unique and precious, crystallizes inside me. At his age, you decided my shoulder was more appetizing and soothing than your teething ring. You gummed me, then bit me, and if I would have allowed you, I'm certain you would've nibbled away my shoulder. You taught me how painless your needs were.

The years were greedy with us. They gobbled up my little girl and left a young lady who tried to conceal the child I visioned. On numerous occasions you informed me you were a woman. Even when you became a lawyer, your voicing it was unacceptable evidence. When we marched down the aisle at your wedding, I didn't feel I was giving you away, just adding to our life. And all that has happened since has proven me correct. It was not until I saw you with your child did I see you anew. The happiness in your face when you looked at him. The way you talked and played with him, burying your face in his stomach, entangling your hair in his grasping hands. Both laughing as if laughter were the song of love.

What I saw I never imagined. All the other phases of your life I peeped into your future and glimpsed them before they arrived. Why was it that I never saw you with child? Did I knowingly blind that vision because of its irrefutability: my child would be gone and replaced by a woman? What do I see now when I look at you holding your child? You were never lovelier. You were never more loving. You were never more lovable. You were never more.

I don't know if it is possible for me to love you more. But I do know there is so much for me to love and to know about my love.

Love,

DAD (ALLISON WEST)

Letter from a Wife

I retrace your path in my bare feet
Press my lips against your empty cup
Touch your clothes for now-gone warmth
View each object which your eyes beheld
Write your name and speak the same
I bless each day you elude the pack
Rehearse each word of love we spoke
Recall the vows your eyes declared
Your last touch lingers with me still
I face each day with dragging feet—weary heart
Apart-from-you takes half my strength
The rest I need for waiting.

S. CAROLYN REESE

Love Letter #15

1

Travel lightly wherever
you go, my dear.
whenever you feel the need
of me come softly

with gifts of openness, come
softly before the altar
of iridescent dreams and
irrepressible hopes.

2

O if it were true that
love is never-ending
and death is not the foe
on the last frontier—

your gift is the gift
eternal and I need
never fear again the threat
of hate or war or pain.

CARL COOK

Lindsay Patterson has written extensively about African-American culture, and, in addition to the original *A Rock Against the Wind,* has edited anthologies on African-American theater, film, and literature. He is a professor of Special Programs at New York's Queens College.

The Building Blocks of Writing

AFRICAN-AM[...]

From the foreword by Ruby Dee:

"We need love poems now
more than ever—when the metaphor of
the rock against the wind has become more
a boulder against a whirlwind of apathy
and madness, of bitterness and rage that
threatens to uproot and erase us. We need
love poems now. In these rhythms and
counter-rhythms we are beautiful; we are
vulnerable; we are strong; we are possible;
we are gloriously (and shamefully) human.
We need these bite-sized bits of love:
new/old/true/low-down/forever/don't-love-
you-no-more/woman/man love."

This anthology is a celebration of love—
the one true emotion that can never be
oppressed or denied.

Perigee Books
are published by
The Berkley
Publishing Group

$12.00 U.S.
$17.00 CAN

EAN
9 780399 519826

ISBN 0-399-51982-3

51200>

HENRY DUMAS
PEARL DUNCAN
CLAY A. FIELDING
[RICH]ARD V. FINNEY, JR.
RICHARD D. GORDON
BARBARA-MARIE GREEN
HAZEL CLAYTON HARRISON
MAE JACKSON
HERSCHEL LEE JOHNSON
JALEELAH KARRIEM
SYBIL KEIN
DOROTHY E. KING
DOUGHTRY LONG
HERBERT WOODWARD MARTIN
IRMA McCLAURIN
DEE DEE McNEIL
DOROTHY MEEKINS
HASNA MUHAMMAD
EMILY M. NEWSOME
DARNLEY OSBORNE
PAT PARKER
LINDSAY PATTERSON
EUGENE REDMOND
S. CAROLYN REESE
ELIZABETH I. ROBERTS
CICELY RODWAY
JOHNIE SCOTT
RICHARD W. THOMAS
HILTON A. VAUGHAN
DENNIS RAHIIM WATSON
BEVERLEY WIGGINS WELLS
AL WEST